AN OSTRICH EXPLAINS AND OTHER NONSUCH POEMS

Florence Remmer

Published by PublishingPush.com

Acknowledgements

FOR MY CHILDREN LYNN, LESLIE AND SID

BEST WISHES
PAT BIGGLEBUM

Contents

5 MICE

Oh wouldn't it be nice
To hire five mice
To keep your bedroom tidy?

They could start as a rule
When you leave for school
You could pay their wages on a Friday

For a big lump of cheese
They would work hard to please
Even clean under your bed....WOW!

They would pick up your clothes
The task you hate most
And place all your shoes in a neat row

If this sounds just the thing for you
 Send an email, neatly, to....
MOUSE5@MOUSEVILLA.COM

A SHORT SHARP LESSON

A very fast mole, a dentist no less
Renowned for the speed of his drill
Can extract 50 teeth in 3 seconds or less
And receives great applause for his skill

Can extract 50 teeth in the blink of an eye
A skill he acquired one fraught day......
A piranha sat down in his dentistry chair
Complaining of dental decay

Aye, a piranha sat waiting, its mouth open wide
The mole set to work in great fright
I think he was thinking his hands were at stake
If he didn't work faster than light

I think he was thinking his fingers were gone…
As he pincered with mind boggling speed
O! he learned a swift lesson in pincering fast
This now stands him in good stead indeed

ONE ALL HOLLOWS EVE...

Thirteen moles, a'quaking,
Five nervous cats and I
Were swapping ghosty stories
Beneath a moonlit sky

Deliciously a'scaring…
Each other (as you do)
When suddenly a proper ghost
Came gliding into view!

A proper ghost!, a'floating!
All misty round about
The screaming moles fast tunnelled …
The sighing cats passed out

I myself, a' screaming,
Began a frenzied sprint
A cloud of dust blew up and I've
Been running ever since,

Yours sincerely
A. ROADRUNNER

A SQUARE DEAL

I wonder if we'd feel at home
If faces were not rounded
What if they were
Square instead?
Would we be confounded?

Square wouldn't suit
The high browed folk
Nor those with jaws a' jutting
Nor would it please
The shaving Man
With all that corner cutting.

And what about the double-chinned?
A' concertined more or less!
NO, the only one
At home would be
The Hammer-headed Shark I guess.

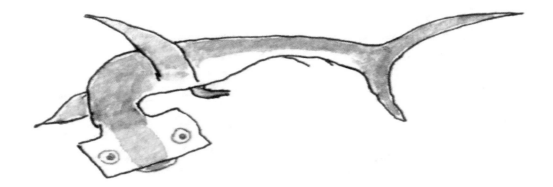

THE DISRESPECTFUL PAWN

A militant Pawn was told to attack
He questioned the order
And moved a step back

Yup he moved a step back, then 3 to the right
This angered the Queen
And startled the Knight

He startled the Knight with a militant look
Then zig-zagged the Bishop
And challenged the Rook

He challenged the Rook
And with Kasparov ease
3 moves to B4 brought the King to his knees

Brought the King to his knees
And to cries of 'shame, shame'
He shouted CHECKMATE and ended the game

AN OSTRICH EXPLAINS

They say we timid ostriches,
When things get out of hand,
Turn our backs and bury
Our heads beneath the sand

Let's hear it for the ostrich! Why?
Our peering into holes
Has less to do with timorous
And more to do with moles

Aye, we peer to watch the busy moles
A'digging down below
We often chill and have a chat
They're friendly, as you know

So, next time you see two ostrich legs…

Fine feathers, but no head,
You'll know the owner, far from shy,
Is a'chilling, (like I've said)

BOO

Two little owls, afraid of the dark,
Sit holding hands every night.
One looks to the left
For signs of... who knows?
And one keeps his eyes to the right.

Some say they're afraid of a rustling leaf,
Some say it's the chattering mice,
But I'm sure it's the moths
Fur coated, you know……..
The ones with the shiny red eyes.

Whatever the reason, those two little owls
Eavesdrop every night in their nest,
One harks to the right,
For sounds of... who knows?
And one bends his ears to the left.

THE LAZY BEE

A very lazy laid back bee
Gently gliding in the sun
Refused to busy buzz about
Refused to do the honey run

Refused to fill the honey pot
Refused to whiz and do his share
The other bees hummed 'tut tut tut'
But he was too laid back to care

The Honey Queen was so enraged
When told about that lazy bee…
She hid the honey pot and left
A dry crust only for his tea

Z Z Z

THE CAT AND THE TREE TRUNK

 A Cat passed by an old Oak Tree
On his daily walk, one Friday
"Good morning and how do you do?"
The Tree enquired politely

"I'm very well," the Cat replied
And carried on a'walking
When a sudden thought came to his mind
How come a Tree was talking?

"Sir, did you speak?" he asked in awe
The Tree replied, "Indeed!
Now run and tell your friends you were
A' talking to a Tree"

The Cat sped off to spread the news
Whilst in a hedge nearby
A Ventriloquist Mouse rolled over
And laughed until he cried

AN OTTER

An Otter on a river bank
(A splendid sight to see)
Dived into the water
Oh, he jack knifed perfectly

Two passing Frogs were watching
And the Otter, being vain,
Climbed back up the river bank
And jack-knifed once again

The passing Frogs applauded
And the Otter, feeling proud,
Ran back up the river bank
And jack-knifed upside down!

THE FOURTEEN FOOLISH MICE

As fourteen Mice set off one night
Looking for some fun
They chanced upon a sleeping Cat,
A mean, long whiskered one

One daring Mouse suggested
(Foolhardy, to be sure)
They use the Cats long whiskers
For a game of 'Tug o' War'

Stifling back their sniggers
They flanked him left and right
And grabbing well the whiskers
Pulled with all their might

The Cat awoke thus pinioned,
And writhed in helpless rage,
Whilst the tugging teams tugged tighter…
Too scared to disengage!

THE MAN WITH AMBIDEXTROUS HANDS

A very clever learned man
With an ambidextrous bent
Could pen a book in half a day
A most prolific gent

Could pen a book in half a day!
His right hand wrote with speed
His left hand checked for errors
Oh, a double act indeed

One day the right hand penned a word
Too vague to understand
The left hand got frustrated
And nipped the erring hand

The right hand nipped it back, but hard
The left hand writhed in pain
And jabbed the right hand with a pen
O, the right hand went insane
And the man thought he was going mad
He never penned a book again.

THE COBBLER

An innovative Mole,
A Cobbler by trade,
Invented a shoe for the one footed Snail.

The Snails being footsore,
Formed a long queue
To purchase the Cobblers one footed shoe

The Mole realized
As the sale gathered speed
He'd forgotten to cater for Snails with left feet

The right footed Snails
Bought up the lot
Delighted to have a shoe for their foot

Whilst the left footed Snails
Went on their way
Grumbling and shoeless I'm sorry to say.

SILENCE IN COURT...

My Client…
The pot bellied pig,
Is here to proclaim
That from here on and henceforth
He is changing his name.
From here on and henceforth
He wishes to be
Officially known
As Mr. P B

For I'm sure you'll agree,
When all's said and done
To be known as 'pot belly'
Is really not on.
Yup, a change of his name
Hopefully sought
By my pot bellied client…OOPS!!…

SILENCE IN COURT!!!

THE GNATS TALE

I acrobat
Round field and wood
But folks are so unkind!!

They shrug and say
It's just a gnat!!
And pay no never mind…

Look

Just because I am a gnat
Doesn't mean
I'm nothing

I'm six times smaller
Than my legs
And that must count
For something
Innit?

THE G.P.

There was a fierce Polecat,
A doctor by trade,
Who refused to kow-tow to illness and pain

Any plea for a sick note
Sent him berserk!!
Why, he'd beat up the culprit and chase him to work!

And as for the housebound
Who dared call him out!!!
He'd fast run to their home to deliver a clout!

Folks say he would lurk
In his rooms…with a club!
Ready to beat anyone who turned up.

Thus his waiting room's empty
His patients are nil
But this he puts down
To his doctoring skill

DEAR AGONY AUNT...

One of my employees,
A malingering, lazy cat,
Feigns sickness every other day
(Of course it's all an act)

Headache (that's a favourite)
Rabies, Tic, Mouse flu.
Yet he's always well on paydays!
Pray tell me what to do
Boss@cheeseshop.com

Dear wronged fed up employer
The answer's very clear…
Hire a Death Watch Beetle
To sit by his bed, my dear

A ticking Death Watch Beetle,
O, the cat will never sleep!
And the shock will send him back to work
Five full days a week.
Mick@agonyaunt.

HUMM HUMM

Now who is the cleverest bird in the world?
Well, if I had to choose one at random….
The humming bird, dear
He sips nectar I hear
As he hums and reverses in tandem

Clever that!

THAT TREE IS DEAD

That tree is dead
Someone said
We'll chop it down tomorrow
"But we're inside"
The wood lice cried
And hung their heads in Sorrow

"Hey we're inside"
The wood lice cried
"And no place else to go"
But by the morrow
They were gone
Where to, I do not know

A LECTURE BY PROFESSOR THOM

To change the Fly Traps' preference
From flies to pesky mice
First zap it with a laser gun
(A brain washing device)

Next, agitate the atoms
In the Fly Traps' tracking zone
For this I use a bigglepren
(An invention of my own)

Then apply the Brownian theory
(Using larger seeds of course)
This will stimulate mouse molecules
In the Venus Fly Traps' nose

By following this formula
You will hear, without a doubt,
Squabbling mice in the Venus trap
All fighting to get out (snigger).

A CAT'S TALE

Dear Manx cat
We notice that
You do not have a Tail?
Oh, I lost it on
A fishing trip…
A'fishing in a Gale

Dear Manx cat
We notice that
You do not
Seem to mind?
No… I find it now
Much easier
To sit
On my behind…….It's more refined

A LOVELY SCARECROW

A kind and gentle Scarecrow
A'poled to the ground
Feeds the birds and rabbits
When the Farmer aint around

Yes a kind and friendly scarecrow
With a bowler on his head
Shares the peas and turnips
When the Farmer is a'bed

And through the snowy winter
In his pockets stuffed with straw
He hides nine little field mice
And the Farmer doesn't know

Aww bless xx

A MUSING MAGGOT

I don't know why
But it is so
Dimples on some faces grow

Some faces sport
Two sparkling eyes
On others lashes, curly, rise

Some faces raise
An eyebrow, fine,
None of these goodies grow on mine

Now can this be
The reason why
Folks turn away when I slide by?

SONG OF THE V. VAIN WALNUT

"Oh bring me a mirror
And let me see
What the Botox man
 Has done for me"

"It cost a bomb,
I'll give you that
But now I'm all so
Wrinkle free"

So sang the V. Vain Walnut
"My, don't I look a treat?"
(But what a passing Peanut said
I really can't repeat!)

THE SONG OF THE TRAP DOOR CRAB

tra la la
As a very old Crab
Sat in his house
His memory started to go

...and he couldn't recall
If the door on his Trap
Swung open a'to or a'fro

No he couldn't recall
The swing of his Trap
And sat there imprisoned for days

'Til a turn of the tide
Swished open his door
Whence he ran out and scurried away
Folderoo tra la la folderay

TALKING TO HIMSELF

A cat was talking to himself
(He thought he was alone)
 "I think I'll take a walk," he said
And answered, "Stay at home...

You know the weather's turning cold"
"So what?" The cat replied,
"I'll go out if I want to"
"Oh no you won't," he cried...

The cat became quite vocal
Exchanging angry words
When suddenly he noticed
He was being overheard...

He spied two mice a'giggling
Soft sniggering... whereupon
He gave a red faced sheepish grin
And feigned a humming song.

ONE MAD MARCH DAY

A daredevil Dog,
May his courage prevail,
Decided to swing
From a tree by his tail.

An eccentric Tom Cat,
With a whoop and a holler,
Decided to swing
From the Dog by his collar.

A freeloading Mouse,
And two passing Fleas,
All decided to swing
From the Cat by her knees.

O, they swung in the sunshine
With nary a care,
And for all that I know
They are still swinging there.

THE AMBITIOUS WEATHERCOCK

A hard working bod
Mr B. Cockerel
With a martial arts glint in his eye
Worked as a weathervane
Six days a week
On his day off he tackled Muay Thai

On his day off he tackled
Muay Thai and the such
(That's scrapping, you know,
With the feet)
And he twizzled and Muay Thai'd
His way to the top
A determined young cockerel indeed!

Yes he twizzled and Muay Thai'd
His way to the top
Now he's cock of the ring,
I've heard tell
And he out kicks them all
At celebrity bouts
And he goes by the fight name of
WEATHER VANE BILL!!!!!

SHAME

The organ grinder's monkey
Must feel a rank outsider
Folks don't want to speak to him
They want the organ grinder

AWW !!

THE ANTS AND THE CAT

An army of ants marched over a fence
Searching for sugar (and anything else)
A cat lay snoozing in their course
They carried on marching with nary a pause

Aye, they carried on marching with nary a rest
Up the cats tail and over his chest
Up the cat's chest and over his back…
They carried on marching in search of a snack

The cat gently stirred as the army marched by
And turned on his back, and opened one eye….
…When he saw what he saw, he fainted with fear
And lost one of his lives, you'll be sorry to hear

A MUSICAL TRIO

A musical trio, two mice and a cat,
Play fine music at parties, you know, do's like that.
The mice play the fiddles with rhythm and flair
And the cat sings the songs with a dignified air

An aloof little trio, appearing quite proud
Why, the mention of money was NEVER allowed
(But a hat for donations was placed, half discreet
In a spotlighted spot by the cats trembling feet

And those fiddling mice and the fine tenored cat
With three eyes on each other and three on the hat
Play fine music at weddings but sorry to say
Fur flies round that hat the end of the day

THE BRAVE AND INNOVATIVE BARBER

A bad tempered Lion King
Sat on his throne
And decided his hair was in need of a comb.

He summoned nine Barbers,
But only one came.
The rest were too frightened (and you'd feel the same).

The Brave one turned up
With a long garden rake
And shinned up a tree, for his own safety's sake.

He clung to the tree
As he swung to and fro.
And he combed out the mane of the Lion below.

The King was amused…
He unsharpened his claws
And I think the brave Barber deserves our applause.

THE ELF WHO PAINTS FLAMINGOS PINK

The elf who paints flamingos pink
Decided she would ask
A chappie from the Walrus Clan
To help her in her task

She hired an arty walrus
Who, unbeknown to her,
Was a little out of kilter;
(An eccentric, as it were)

Now, flamingos look unvarious
The Walrus thought so too,
He planned a dab of rainbow paint
To variegate their hue.

But the Elf who paints flamingos,
Appalled at such a plan,
Sent the "would be different" back
To the Walrus Clan.

THE KNOWLEDGEABLE SEA HORSE

A shimmering silvery mermaid
Grabbed me by my toe
And asked of me a favour
Before she let me go

She asked of me a favour….
Would I help her in her quest?
She was searching for an oyster
With an emerald in its breast

An emerald clutching oyster?
O, that's easy mermaid! …down
In Davy Jones's locker
Such a treasure can be found

Aye, in Davy Jones's locker
Beneath the South Sea's swell
There lives an ancient oyster
With an emerald in its shell

THE AMBITIOUS SPIDER...

…who made a living
Spinning silk
To sell from door to door…
…who bought herself
A spinning wheel
So she could spin the more…

…who soon became
Quite affluent,
And, desirous of the best,…
… bought four and twenty
Chains of gold
To string around her web!.

Bought six and forty
Lustrous pearls…
…full thirty emeralds green
And etched her
Busy spinning aide
In silver filigree…

Who proud displayed

Her luring home
 In all is lustrous state...
        ...to thirteen envious Bower Birds
        Who vowed to emulate.

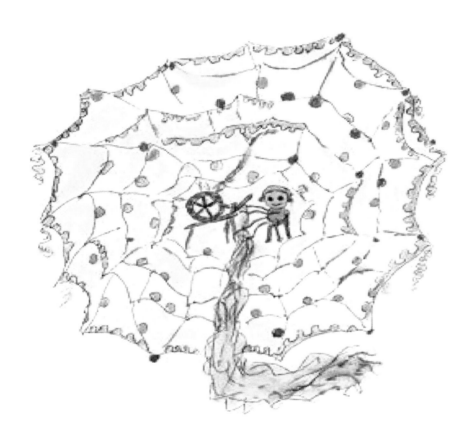

A SAGEFUL TURKEY

Turkey please tell me just how you've been able
To avoid ending up on a Christmassy table
Why, you must be 100, so fit and alive!
O, how have you managed
So long
To survive?

Well…I ready myself when September draws near
To go on the strictest of diets my dear
Oh the barest of diets, no doubt about that
Then when Christmas draws near
I'm as thin
As a lath

Yes, when Christmas arrives I get left in my pen
'Cos who wants to buy a scraggy thin hen?
I've been working this flanker most of my life
And that
In a nutshell
Is how I've survived.

A COCKLE'S COMPLAINT

One moonlit night…
…wearing lots of silvery shoes
And jostling on the sands
Fifteen crabs in merry mode
Were dancing hand in hand

Fifteen crabs a'scuttling
In a laughing mad array
Why, had I pair of silvery shoes
I'd surely with them sway!

Peering from my cockle shell
I watched the moonlight gleam
On fifteen crabs a'roistering
On madly dancing feet

But sharp their spell was broken
When, scuttling here and there,
They trod upon my little shell
Too merrified to care.

THE NEW SHOAL SCHOOL

We gathered all together
As eager as herrings can be
We took a roll call
Ere they taught us to shoal
Round and up through the silvery sea

We started well together!
Down where the mermaids dwell,
See us sway left and right
In the eerie green light,
To the booms of the ocean swell

We're curving well together
In a spiralling silvery swirl
See us sway with a swoop
Swooping round in a loop
To and fro in a bubbling whirl.

Oh, we schooled well together…
And they gave us a herring degree!
Our learning was fun
Now we're shoaling as one
Teeming proud through the welcoming sea.

Printed in Great Britain
by Amazon